Ladybird Readers

Grimlock Stops
the Decepticons

COVENTRY LIBRARIES
WITHDRAWN
FOR SALE

COVENTRY LIBRARIES
WITHDRAWN
FOR SALE

3 8002 02359 310 8

Coventry City Council	
WIL	
3 8002 02359 310 8	
Askews & Holts	Feb-2018
BEGINNER READER	£4.99

Series Editor: Sorrel Pitts

Adapted by Hazel Geatches

LADYBIRD BOOKS

UK | USA | Canada | Ireland | Australia
India | New Zealand | South Africa

Ladybird Books is part of the Penguin Random House group of companies
whose addresses can be found at global.penguinrandomhouse.com.
www.penguin.co.uk   www.puffin.co.uk   www.ladybird.co.uk

Penguin
Random House
UK

First published 2018
001

HASBRO and its logo, TRANSFORMERS, TRANSFORMERS ROBOTS IN DISGUISE, the logo and all related
characters are trademarks of Hasbro and are used with permission.
© 2018 Hasbro. All Rights Reserved.

Licensed by:

Printed in China

A CIP catalogue record for this book is available from the British Library

ISBN: 978-0-241-31954-3

All correspondence to
Ladybird Books
Penguin Random House Children's
80 Strand, London WC2R 0RL

MIX
Paper from
responsible sources
FSC® C018179

Ladybird Readers

Grimlock Stops the Decepticons

Picture words

Denny

 Russell

Autobots

Bumblebee

Strongarm

Grimlock

Fixit

Simacore
(a Decepticon)

Minicons

scrapyard

laboratory

scanner

Bumblebee and Strongarm were in the scrapyard.

"We have a big problem," said Strongarm.

"The Decepticons want to take things from the laboratory. We must stop them," she said.

Grimlock came into the scrapyard, and heard them.

"I can stop the Decepticons," he said.

"No, it's OK, Grimlock," said Bumblebee and Strongarm.

Grimlock was very sad.
He went to see Russell
and Denny.

"What's the matter, Grimlock? Why are you sad?" asked Denny.

"Bumblebee and Strongarm don't want me to help," said Grimlock. "They are clever, but I am not."

"You are big and strong. That is good, too," said Russell.

"Oh no!" said Fixit. "The Decepticons are in the laboratory. I can see them on my scanner!"

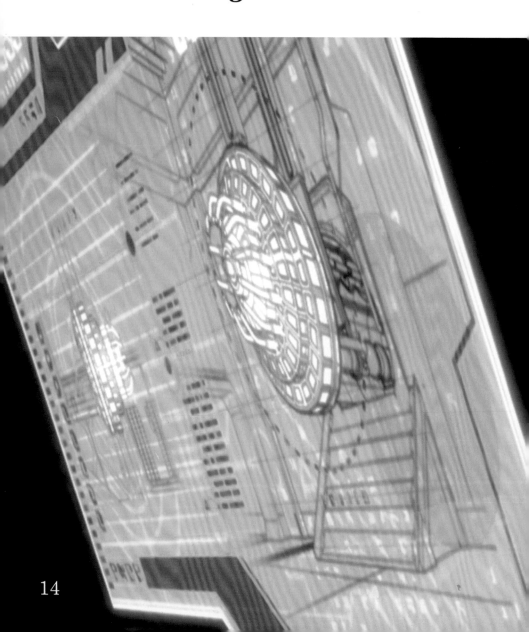

"Who can you see?"
asked Bumblebee.

"I can see Simacore and
two Minicons," said Fixit.

"Strongarm, we must go to the laboratory and stop the Decepticons," said Bumblebee.

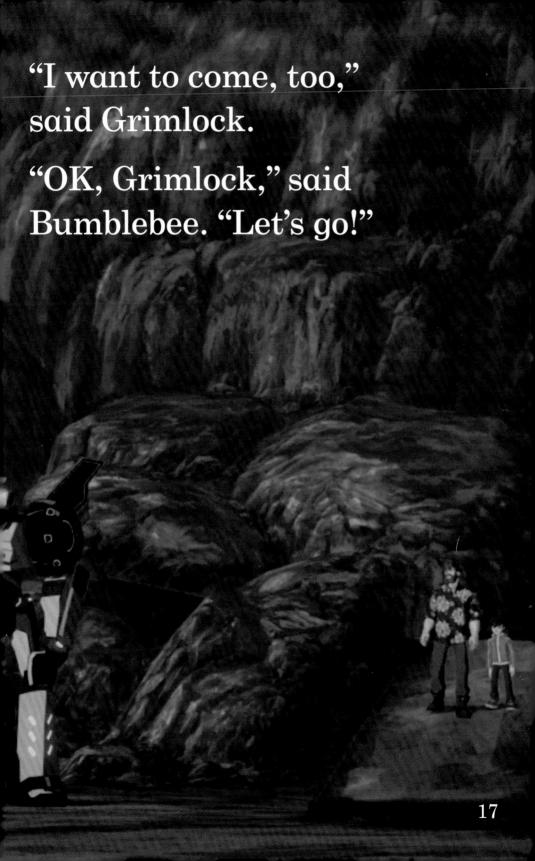

"I want to come, too,"
said Grimlock.

"OK, Grimlock," said
Bumblebee. "Let's go!"

Strongarm, Bumblebee,
and Grimlock ran quickly
to the laboratory.

"What's in here?"
asked Strongarm.

"There are many important things in this laboratory," said Bumblebee. "The Decepticons want to take them."

The Autobots went inside the laboratory. There, Simacore waited for them.

"Good evening, Autobots," he said.

"Stay there!" said Strongarm.

"No! You can't catch me!" said Simacore.

Then, two Minicons flew at the Autobots.

Bumblebee and Strongarm ran quickly at the Minicons. They hit them, and they kicked them.

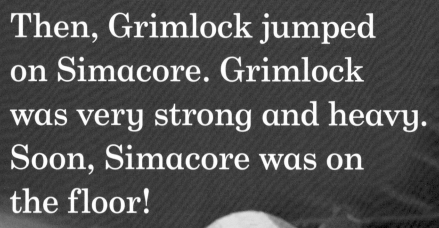

Then, Grimlock jumped on Simacore. Grimlock was very strong and heavy. Soon, Simacore was on the floor!

Bumblebee, Strongarm,
and Grimlock went back
to the scrapyard.

"Thank you, Grimlock!"
said Bumblebee.

"You are very strong, Grimlock," said Strongarm.

"Well done, Grimlock!" said Russell, Denny, and Fixit.

Now, Grimlock was very happy.

Activities

The key below describes the skills practiced in each activity.

🖊 Spelling and writing

📖 Reading

💬 Speaking

❓ Critical thinking

✴ Preparation for the Cambridge Young Learners exams

Match the words to the pictures.

1 Grimlock

a

b

2 Strongarm

c

3 Simacore

d

4 Minicons

2 **Look and read. Choose the correct words, and write them on the lines.** 📖 ✏️ ❁ ❓

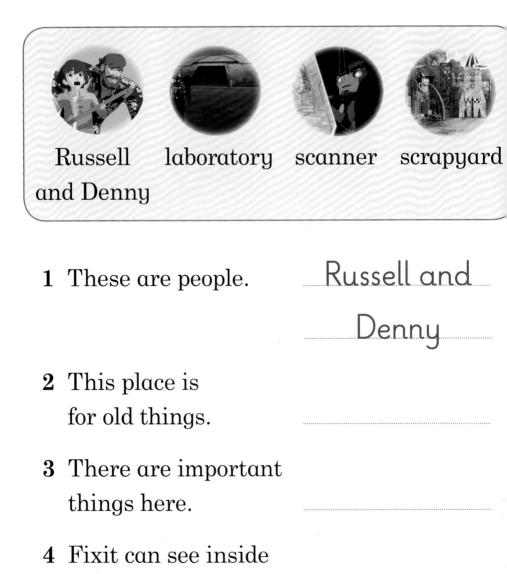

Russell and Denny   laboratory   scanner   scrapyard

1 These are people.

Russell and Denny

2 This place is for old things.

3 There are important things here.

4 Fixit can see inside places with this.

3 Circle the correct words.

Bumblebee and Strongarm were in the scrapyard.

"We have a big problem," said Strongarm.

"The Decepticons want to take things from the laboratory. We must stop them," she said.

1 Where is Bumblebee?

a the laboratory (**b** the scrapyard)

2 Who is with Bumblebee?

a Strongarm **b** Decepticons

3 What do the Decepticons want to take from the laboratory?

a things **b** people

4 Who has to stop the Decepticons?

a Simacore **b** the Autobots

Look and read. Write *yes* or *no*.

Grimlock came into the scrapyard, and heard them.

"I can stop the Decepticons," he said.

"No, it's OK, Grimlock," said Bumblebee and Strongarm.

1 Grimlock came into the scrapyard.

........yes........

2 Grimlock heard Bumblebee and Strongarm.

....

3 "I can stop you," said Grimlock.

....

4 "I can stop the Decepticons," said Grimlock.

....

5 Bumblebee and Strongarm wanted Grimlock to help.

....

Denny   Grimlock   Russell

1 "What's the matter, Grimlock? Why are you sad?" asked

Denny .

2 "Bumblebee and Strongarm don't want me to help," said

.

3 "They are clever," said

.

4 "You are big and strong. That is good, too," said

.

35

6 Read the questions.
Write the answers.

Bumblebee and Strongarm were in the scrapyard.

"We have a big problem," said Strongarm.

"The Decepticons want to take things from the laboratory. We must stop them," she said.

1 Who had a problem?

The Autobots had a problem.

2 Did the Autobots like the Decepticons?
Why? / Why not?

....

....

3 Why did the Decepticons go to
the laboratory?

....

....

Talk to a friend about Grimlock.

1 Is Grimlock blue?

No, he's green and black.

2 What does Grimlock want to do?

3 Why is Grimlock sad?

4 What do you know about Grimlock?

Circle the correct sentences.

"Oh no!" said Fixit. "The Decepticons are in the laboratory. I can see them on my scanner!"

"Who can you see?" asked Bumblebee.

"I can see Simacore and two Minicons," said Fixit.

1 a Fixit saw the Decepticons in the laboratory.

b The Decepticons took the scanner.

2 a "Who can you see?" asked Simacore.

b "Who can you see?" asked Bumblebee.

3 a Fixit could see Simacore and two Minicons.

b Bumblebee could see Simacore and two Minicons.

9 **Ask and answer the questions with a friend.**

1

> *Who did Fixit see on his scanner?*

> *He saw the Decepticons.*

2 Why were the Decepticons in the laboratory?

3 Did Bumblebee want Grimlock to help?

4 How did Grimlock help his friends?

10 Circle the correct words.

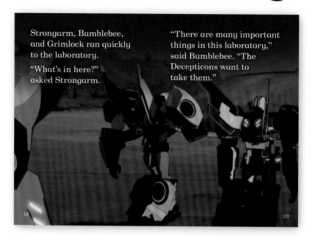

Strongarm, Bumblebee, and Grimlock ran quickly to the laboratory.

"What's in here?" asked Strongarm.

"There are many important things in this laboratory," said Bumblebee. "The Decepticons want to take them."

1 Bumblebee, Strongarm, and Grimlock ran to the **scrapyard. / laboratory.**

2 **Bumblebee / Strongarm** asked, "What's in here?"

3 "There are many important **people / things** in this laboratory," said Bumblebee.

4 "The **people / Decepticons** want to take them," said Bumblebee.

11 Find the words.

kdf l a b o r a t o r y m u N i n i c o n s g r e M r s s c a n n e r t i p s c r a p y a r d S u n S i m a c o r e l

laboratory

scrapyard

scanner

Simacore

Minicons

12 Look and read. Put a ☑ or a ☒ in the boxes.

1  The Autobots had to stop the Decepticons. ✓

2  They ran quickly to the laboratory.

3  "There are many important things here," said Strongarm.

4  Simacore saw Strongarm, and he was happy.

5  Two Minicons helped Simacore.

13 **Complete the sentences.**
Write a—d.

1 The Autobots went ....b........

2 There, Simacore ....

3 "You can't catch me!" ....

4 Two Minicons ....

a waited for them.

b inside the laboratory.

c flew at the Autobots.

d said Simacore.

14 Write the correct words.

1 Bumblebee and Strongarm **(run)**

_____ran_____ quickly at the Minicons.

2 They **(kick)** _____ them.

3 They **(hit)** _____ them.

4 Then, Grimlock **(jump)**

_____ on Simacore.

5 Soon, Simacore **(be)** _____ on the floor.

15 Do the crossword.

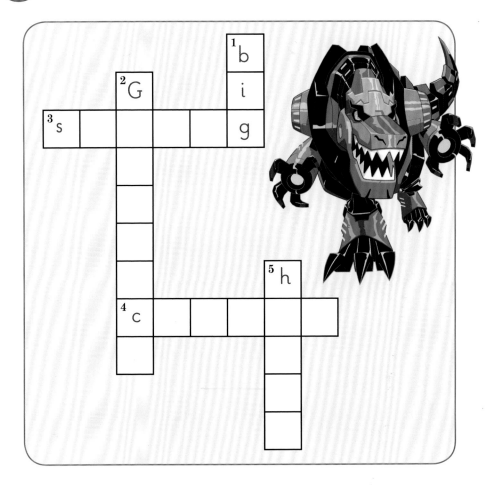

Down

1 "You are . . . and strong."

2 . . . wanted to help.

5 Grimlock was very strong and . . .

Across

3 Grimlock was very . . . and heavy.

4 Grimlock told Denny, "I am not . . ."

16 **Write the correct questions.**

1 to   Who   the   went
scrapyard   back   ?

Who went back to

the scrapyard?

2 say   What   to   did
Grimlock?   Strongarm

....

....

3 "Well done!"   Who   to
said   Grimlock   ?

....

....

17 **Draw a picture of an Autobot. Read the questions and write the answers.** 📖 ✏️ ❓

1 What is the name of your Autobot?

My Autobot is

2 What can your Autobot do?

3 How does your Autobot help you?

Level 2

The Gingerbread Man

978-0-241-25442-4

Sly Fox and Red Hen

978-0-241-25443-1

The Monster Next Door

978-0-241-25444-8

Wild Animals

978-0-241-25445-5

Little Red Riding Hood

978-0-241-25446-2

Dinosaurs

978-0-241-25447-9

Topsy and Tim The Big Race

978-0-241-25448-6

Goes to the Treehouse

978-0-241-25449-3

Sports Day

978-0-241-26222-1

Going on a Picnic

978-0-241-26221-4

Peter Rabbit and the Angry Owl

978-0-241-28369-1

Superhero Max

978-0-241-28368-4

We Can Help!

978-0-241-28367-7

Daddy Pig's New Van

978-0-241-28371-4

School Trip

978-0-241-28372-1

The Peter Rabbit Club

978-0-241-29811-4

Daddy Pig's Office

978-0-241-29814-5

Spring is Here!

978-0-241-29809-1

Great Trains

978-0-241-29808-4

Hungry Animals

978-0-241-29844-2

Playing Football

978-0-241-31947-5

In a Plane

978-0-241-31945-1

Mountains

978-0-241-31948-2

Grimlock Stops the Decepticons

978-0-241-31954-3

Now you're ready for Level 3!